The Biting Cheese Bows Challenge

Navy Dad Series - Book 1

Kathleen Thaler

Illustrated by Mike Carter

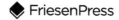 FriesenPress

Suite 300 - 990 Fort St
Victoria, BC, V8V 3K2
Canada

www.friesenpress.com

Copyright © 2017 by Kathleen Thaler
First Edition — 2017

All rights reserved.

No part of this publication may be reproduced in any form, or by any means, electronic or mechanical, including photocopying, recording, or any information browsing, storage, or retrieval system, without permission in writing from FriesenPress.

ISBN
978-1-4602-8127-7 (Hardcover)
978-1-4602-8128-4 (Paperback)
978-1-4602-8129-1 (eBook)

1. JUVENILE FICTION, MYSTERIES &
DETECTIVE STORIES

Distributed to the trade by The Ingram Book Company

Table of Contents

THE CHARACTERS

Abbey

Alice

Tommy Tucker

Twinkles

CHAPTER 1

CHEESE CHALLENGE

"GOOD MORNING, TWINKLES" ABBEY whispered to her pet hamster as she stretched and got out of bed.

Suddenly, she noticed something long and skinny on the floor.

"Eeek!" she cried as she jumped back on the bed.

When she peeked over the edge of the bed, Twinkles said, "I don't think it's a snake. While I was exercising in my wheel last night, working off those blueberries you gave me, which were delicious actually - "

"Get to the *point*, Twinkles!" Abbey exclaimed.

"Oh yes, right. Well, your dad came in and put that thing on the floor, then put a note on your bedside table, and then kissed you on the forehead before leaving." Twinkles always explained things in great detail.

Abbey turned on her lamp and saw the note left by her dad. Unfolding it, she read:

Hi Honey,
I will be away at sea for 5 days and I thought you might like a TOP SECRET SUPER DUPER CHALLENGE. There is a surprise box waiting for you at the end if you complete the 3 steps.

See you soon,
Love, Dad xox

"Oooh, Twinkles! Isn't this exciting?" Abbey squealed.

She thought about her dad at sea on his Navy ship and how he always left her *nautical* challenges when he was away. Last time, he left her a challenge about bunks, which is the nautical way of saying beds. Sometimes he would be away for months and the challenges would be long, but this time she only had five days to figure things out! She had no time to lose, she had to get started right away.

Abbey ran over to the object on the floor and saw that it was a long, braided rope, just a bit thicker than her skipping rope. There was a pink sticky note on one end that read:

"Cheese? Did someone say cheese?" asked Twinkles excitedly.

"Yup. That's what it says. Maybe we should check the fridge for another clue? C'mon, Twinkles." Abbey placed the hamster in her pyjama shirt pocket and headed to the kitchen.

"So what kind of cheese do you think we need, Twinkles?" Abbey asked while pulling a few choices out of the deli drawer. "*Blue cheese*? Nah, too stinky." She put that one back.

"Cheddar maybe? Or Swiss?" Twinkles poked his head out of the pocket and his eyes lit up at the sight of all the cheese in front of them.

"Maybe we should sit and have a piece of each one of them while we think about it," he answered. "I always think better on a full stomach." He smiled his cutest smile and twitched his whiskers.

Abbey smiled back and cut a small piece of marble Cheddar for him. "I just don't know what cheese has to do with this rope. This sure is a **TOP SECRET SUPER DUPER CHALLENGE**!"

Abbey headed to her room to get dressed for school. She quickly brushed her blonde hair, but it still stuck out on the sides when she was done. *'Good enough'* she thought as she put on her most comfy pants, with big cargo pockets on the sides. She liked to wear these for adventures since she never knew when she would have to pick up a clue along the way.

She thought about her dad at sea, and giggled when she imagined him using ropes made of cheese onboard. Yum, cheese strings.

CHAPTER
2

BITE ME

SITTING DOWN FOR BREAKFAST, ABBEY saw another rope on her placemat. This one was much shorter, only the length of her elbow to her fingertips. Looking closer, a little green sticky note read:

"Yuck! Who wants to eat a rope?" Twinkles asked with disgust.

"I'm not sure that's what it means. Plus, bight is spelled wrong."

At that moment, Abbey's mother walked in with a knowing look. "Good morning, sweetie. How about some breakfast for my little adventurer?"

"Yes please. Cheese and toast would be great. Dad's notes sure are making me hungry!" Abbey replied. Twinkles twitched his nose in approval. No one else knew that the hamster could talk.

"Mom, do you know what I'm supposed to do with these ropes?" Abbey asked.

"It would spoil your adventure if I gave you the answers. You're in Grade 3 now and I'm sure you can figure it out. Maybe Alice would like to help too?" Abbey's mother suggested as she left the room.

Abbey was suddenly excited to get to school so she could talk to her best friend, Alice. She and Alice had solved a few of Dad's **TOP SECRET SUPER DUPER CHALLENGES** together and Abbey was sure they could tackle this one too. As she ate her breakfast, she considered the small rope on the table.

"Twinkles," she said aloud, "I wonder if you should try just a *nibble*?"

"Why me? Why don't you try a bite instead? Why do I have to be a guinea pig – I'm a hamster you know!"

Abbey gave him a little smile, and answered with a laugh. "Yes, I know you're a hamster, and hamsters nibble on all sorts of stuff. Plus, I just had my breakfast, so I'm a bit full right now."

Twinkles gave in. "Okay, okay. But next time you have fresh blueberries, I hope you give me double the usual amount!"

Twinkles sniffed the tiny rope next to Abbey's plate. "Smells normal," he said. He took a small bite of the end. "Tastes normal – for a rope," he continued. But nothing happened. The rope just sat there.

"I guess *Bight me* is not the same as *Bite me*," Abbey remarked. With that, Abbey headed to get ready for school. She tucked the smallest rope and the two sticky notes into her pants pocket, but decided to leave the long rope at home. She would ask Alice to come over after school to see that one.

After brushing her teeth, she went to get her backpack near the front door and suddenly noticed a small brown box with a rope laying beside it. "The third part of the challenge! Hurray!" she shouted as she rushed forward to see.

CHAPTER 3

THE PERFECT BOW

THE BOX WAS BEAUTIFUL. IT WAS MADE OF wood, with metal corners that looked like gold. Beside it lay a medium sized-rope, with a yellow sticky note this time:

I need a Bowline

"All this box needs is a bow! That's easy-peasy," said Abbey to Twinkles who had *stowed away* in the other cargo pocket. The hamster always tried to sneak its way to school with her.

"Um, not to be a Gloomy Gus, but I think it might take more than a bow. It's supposed to be a challenge, right?" Twinkles replied.

Abbey made a face and answered, "I guess you're right. I'd better put this note in my pocket too." Then she picked up the box to examine it more closely. There was a mini lock on it, with a tiny scroll of paper sticking out of the keyhole. Unrolling the paper, Abbey read:

Abbey,
You now have 3 ropes and 3 clues to get you started on your adventure. Once you have figured out what to do with each rope, bring it to your mom to check. When all 3 are completed, you will get the key to this box as a reward. Good luck! See you in 5 days.
Love Dad
P.S. I love you knots, oh, I mean lots!

She stuffed the note in her pocket with the others. Not much more would fit. There was no time to think about it yet since she had to catch the bus. She raced to put Twinkles back in his cage, grabbed her favourite sneakers, and headed for the door. Ever since she had started Grade 3 she was allowed to walk to the bus stop at the corner of her street by herself. It was a very grown-up thing to do.

"Bye, Mom, see you later!" she called as she went out. On her way to the bus stop, she could feel the small rope in her pocket banging against her leg.

'Cheese, bight, bowline,' she said to herself. What do these have in common? All of Dad's past challenges had to do with the Navy, so Abbey was sure this one would too.

On the bus, Abbey pulled out the notes and read through them again. But when Tommy Tucker looked over the seat to see what she was doing, she quickly stuffed the notes back into her baggy pocket. This was a **TOP SECRET SUPER DUPER CHALLENGE** that she would only share with Alice. It was *not* meant for nosy Tommy Tucker.

Oh, why couldn't the bus go faster?

CHAPTER
4

A KNOTTY PLOT

ABBEY GOT OFF THE BUS AND RAN TO find Alice in the play yard.

"Alice! Alice! I have exciting news for you!" she yelled as she got closer. "My dad left on his ship this morning, so you know what that means don't you?"

Alice's green eyes grew wide with excitement. "**A TOP SECRET SUPER DUPER CHALLENGE**?" Alice asked hopefully.

"Yes, and this one is really tricky. It has to do with biting cheese bows."

Alice made a funny face. "What? Biting cheese bows? Maybe I should look at the clue too. Two heads are better than one."

"Actually, there are 3 clues and an instruction note," Abbey explained. "Let's go find a quiet corner so I can show you everything."

On a bench away from everyone, Abbey pulled the rope and notes from her pocket. She told Alice about each different sized rope and described the wooden box with the little lock. When she finished her tale, she could tell Alice was as excited as she was.

"Okay, let's review what we know for sure," Alice suggested.

"Well, we know that the challenges involve rope and that they probably have to do with the Navy somehow," Abbey began.

"And we know that each challenge takes a different sized rope," Alice continued.

Abbey suddenly had an idea. "There's not much written on the clues, but maybe there's a hidden clue on the instruction note? Dad can be tricky like that sometimes. Remember the clue he left us in the 'Bunk Challenge' last year?" Both girls giggled, remembering how Abbey's father had put a clue into the note, right there in front of them the whole time! Once they realized it, the whole puzzle was solved.

"Alice, can you read the note out loud? After each sentence we'll stop and see if there might be a hidden clue."

Alice took the instruction note and began to read. *"Abbey, you now have 3 ropes and 3 clues to get you started on your adventure."* Alice read with a smile.

"Hey, what if the clue is the word '*adventure*'? Maybe it means we have to go somewhere," suggested Abbey.

"Hmm, that's an idea," said Alice, "but where should we go?"

The girls decided to keep reading the note in case there was another clue.

Alice continued reading. *"Once you have figured out what to do with each rope, bring it to Mom to check."*

Abbey grinned and said, "We have to do something with each rope separately. Nothing too big or we'd never get it back to Mom."

Alice scrunched up her face, thinking. "What can we do with rope? Twist it, pull on it, skip with it, tie it to something, or make something out of it?"

"Well, we can't make cheese out of it, and we can't bite it. We *can* make a bow with it, but a bowline might be different," Abbey said miserably.

Alice kept reading out loud: "*When all 3 are completed, you will get the key to this box as a reward. Good luck! See you in 5 days.*"

Both girls were quiet for a moment before Abbey said, "I don't see any clue in that part, unless it has to do with the numbers 3 and 5."

"Maybe," Alice replied, "but all I know is 5 days isn't long at all to figure this out."

Both girls were disappointed that no obvious clues seemed to be in the note. They were *stumped*.

"You may as well read the PS. at the bottom of the note," Abbey suggested without enthusiasm.

Alice looked down and read, *"PS. I love you knots, oh, I mean lots!"* Both girls looked at each other with sudden excitement – knots! And then the school bell rang.

CHAPTER 5

TEACHER TALK

OH, OF ALL THE ROTTEN LUCK! JUST WHEN they had a real clue to the challenge, the girls had to sit through math and science classes before recess. Abbey, who normally liked doing multiplication, couldn't concentrate. In science, she was thinking more about knots than about the lifecycle of frogs. When Mrs. Picard, their teacher, asked her about a frog's habitat, Alice had to kick her under the desk to get her attention. But it was too late.

"Abbey, please stay behind at recess," Mrs. Picard directed sternly. "I'd like to speak with you."

Abbey thought about how her luck seemed to be getting worse. Now she wouldn't be able to talk to Alice about the clue until lunchtime.

The recess bell rang and Abbey watched the class go outside without her. She walked up to Mrs. Picard's desk and waited.

"So, Abbey, what has you so distracted today? You are usually one of the most attentive students," Mrs. Picard noted.

Abbey wasn't sure if she should tell her teacher about the **TOP SECRET SUPER DUPER CHALLENGE**. Then, she thought that Dad wouldn't mind if Mrs. Picard knew, as long as she kept the secret. Abbey quickly explained about the challenges Dad left when he as at sea, and showed her the notes and rope stuffed into her cargo pants pocket. She finished by telling Mrs. Picard about the exciting new clue that she and Alice had discovered before class.

"I'm so sorry that I wasn't listening in class," Abbey apologized, "but it's just that this is our first big clue and we only have five days to solve the challenge!" Abbey waited to hear what her punishment would be while she pushed the rope and notes back into her pocket quickly.

Mrs. Picard paused a moment, then smiled. "I will make you a deal. If you really focus on your class work until lunch, I will give you and Alice a special pass for the library. Instead of going outside to play, you can go work on your challenge together. What do you think?"

Abbey wanted to hug her teacher. She was so happy. Instead, she replied, "I *promise* to concentrate on my work. Thank you, thank you, thank you!"

Mrs. Picard nodded and let Abbey head outside for the last few minutes of recess. Maybe her luck was not so bad after all. In fact, it seemed to be getting much better.

When she met Alice outside, she was just about to tell her the good news when Tommy Tucker came over. "Sooooo, it looks like you got into trouble," he said. "Did it have any-thing to do with *this*?" he asked as he pulled the pink sticky note from her cargo pocket and read it. She must not have put the note back in her pocket properly after showing Mrs. Picard!

"Hey! Give that back! It's a secret!" Abbey yelled and tried to grab it. But Tommy held it behind his back.

"A secret, huh? I love secrets. I'm not sure cheese is very secret though. Here." He handed the note back with a sneer. "You girls are crazy." And then he ran off as the bell rang.

Running to get into line, Abbey told Alice about the deal she had made with Mrs.

Picard. No more talk about the challenge until they were in the library. Both girls smiled the whole rest of the morning, even when they had a surprise spelling quiz.

CHAPTER
6

LIBRARY LUCK

AT LUNCH, THE GIRLS TOOK THE SPECIAL pass from Mrs. Picard and walked to the library as fast as school rules allowed. It was only down the hall but it seemed far away today.

When they arrived, they were greeted by Miss Dewey, the librarian. "Good afternoon ladies. What can I help you with today?"

"Knots!" both girls exclaimed at the same time, then giggled.

"You're looking for a book about knots? Any kind of knot in particular?" the librarian asked.

Abbey suggested naval knots, or knots to use on boats. Miss Dewey explained how she used her computer to search for keywords like knot, Navy, and marine. Since the school library was so small, only one book showed up on her screen.

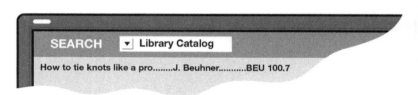

The librarian showed the girls how to use the catalogue system and pointed them to a section in the back corner of the library. Without wasting a minute, the girls started looking through the shelves for the author's last name.

"BEA, BEI, BEO.... Here! BEU!" Abbey yelled, a little more loudly than she had intended. Miss Dewey gave her a look.

Sure enough, the book about knots was right there in front of them. They took it to a reading desk and pulled their chairs together so they could both see.

"We should start with the index," Alice suggested. "We can look up cheese, bight and bowline, and see what we find."

Abbey flipped to the back of the book where the index was. Running her finger down the alphabetical list, she searched for 'bight'. Her smile faded when the word wasn't in the index.

"Back to bad luck I guess," she sighed. "Maybe we were wrong about the clues being related to knots."

The girls looked at each other and Alice said, "Well, we're here already. We may as well look up the other two words."

Abbey nodded and went back to the index. After 'bight' would be 'bowline'…

Just like that, her finger landed on BOWLINE.

"I can't believe it! It's on page 22!" Abbey exclaimed in amazement.

Flipping to that page, the girls found a detailed drawing:

22

Abbey wanted to jump for joy. "This is it! We need to learn how to tie a bowline with the rope my dad left."

Alice looked down at the page and back up at Abbey. "It looks pretty complicated," she said.

"Oh, c'mon Alice, we can do it. I know we can. We just need practice."

"Alright," Alice agreed, "let's see if we can borrow this book to take home with us. But first, let's look up 'cheese' too."

They went back to the index, but there was no mention of cheese. The girls didn't mind so much though, since they had figured out one clue already. They made a plan to meet at Abbey's house after school, where they could practice with the medium-sized rope.

After signing out the book for a week, the girls headed to class for an afternoon of reading and gym. Alice went in to the class while Abbey was putting the book into her locker. As luck would have it, Tommy Tucker poked his head in beside her.

"A book about knots huh? Let me guess – another secret?" Tommy teased.

Abbey slammed the locker closed. "It's none of your business. And besides, the teacher is waiting for us." She turned and started walking away.

Tommy called after her. "You know I'm a knot expert don't you? Maybe I can help if you tell me the secret!"

Abbey heard him but kept on walking. She didn't need Tommy Tucker's help.

CHAPTER 7

TIED IN KNOTS

ALICE'S MOTHER DROPPED HER OFF AT Abbey's house after school.

"Can you stay for supper? Mom's making spaghetti and fresh cheesy bread," Abbey asked her friend. Twinkles poked his head up from the soft cage bedding and twitched his whiskers when he heard that.

"You bet!" answered Alice. "Now let's get started on this **TOP SECRET SUPER DUPER CHALLENGE**!"

Abbey showed Alice the three ropes and the little wooden box. Both girls wondered what the surprise could be.

"I hope it's stickers," Abbey said with her fingers crossed.

"How about fancy erasers or a detective notebook?" suggested Alice.

The girls began shouting out *absurd* items, trying to think of the funniest ones.

"Jelly beans that taste like rainbows!"

"A tiny monkey that jumps up and down!"

"Wait, wait, I know! Cotton balls to stick up Tommy Tucker's nose!" Abbey joked.

Both girls laughed and then turned their attention to the drawing of the bowline.

"Okay, let's give this a go," Abbey said.

On the first try, the girls managed to get tangled up in the rope and tip over onto the carpet. On the second try, Alice's leg ended up tied to the chair! She looked so funny that the girls couldn't stop laughing. The next attempt ended with the rope tied in many small knots that looked nothing like a bowline.

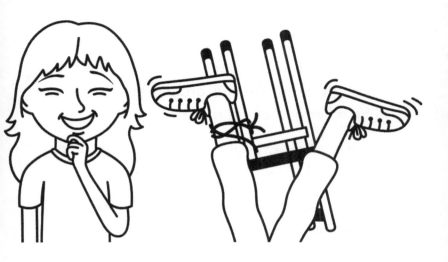

"You know, I've heard my dad say, 'If you don't know knots, tie lots', but this is ridiculous!" Abbey remarked.

Finally, the girls sat down and studied the instructions. "Maybe we should do this slowly, step-by-step," Alice suggested.

The girls read the advice set out by the author: *"A rabbit comes out of the hole, around the tree, and back into the hole"*. When they looked at the picture at the same time as reading this hint, they suddenly understood how to tie the bowline.

First, they made a rabbit's hole by looping the rope over itself.

Second, they brought the rabbit end up through that hole and around the tree trunk (the other end of the rope).

Finally, they brought the rabbit end of the rope back down through the same hole.

Wow. There in front of them was a bowline. They had done it! They looked at each other and back at the rope. It was still there. They shook the rope, but the knot didn't come undone. They had really done it!

"Do you think we should untie it and practice more, until we can do it without the book?" Alice asked.

Even though Abbey was afraid that if they took it apart that they wouldn't be able to tie it again, she agreed.

Carefully, they untied the rope and started again. This time, the bowline was easier to tie. In fact, it got easier each time they did it. By supper time, they were ready to show Abbey's mother what they had learned.

"Mom, watch this. We figured out one of Dad's challenges – the bowline!"

Not only did they show her the knot, but then they tied the bowline around her waist and pulled her around the kitchen by the free end.

"Okay, okay, girls" Mom laughed, "you get a thumbs up for the bowline. Now just two more challenges to go."

Uh-Oh. They were at a dead end. The book said nothing about cheese or bights.

Both girls considered the problem for a moment until Abbey mumbled something that sounded a lot like "Tommy".

"Did you just say 'Tommy'?" Alice asked, surprised.

Abbey took a big breath and nodded. "Yeah, he said he was a knot expert." She rolled her eyes.

Alice shrugged. "Well, we only have 4 days left, so I guess we could ask Tommy for help. As long as he promises not to tell anyone about the **TOP SECRET SUER DUPER CHALLENGE**."

"Do you think we will have to share the treasure in the locked box?" Abbey asked.

"I guess so," Alice replied. Then she smiled. "Unless there are cotton balls in there to shove up his nose!"

Both girls laughed and sat down for the best spaghetti and cheesy bread ever made.

CHAPTER
8

HAMSTER ADVICE

AFTER ALICE HAD GONE HOME, ABBEY went to see Twinkles, who had just woken from his daytime sleep.

"'Twinkles, I have so much to tell you and show you!"

She took out the medium-sized rope and tied a perfect bowline.

"Ta-Da! This is what Dad meant by a bowline," she said with pride.

"That's great! Did you find out anything about the cheese yet? I'm awfully hungry, and cheese sounds perfect."

"Oh Twinkles, you're *always* hungry!" Abbey laughed. She took the hamster out of his cage and placed him on her pillow. She sat down next to him. Her face got serious as she thought about the next day.

"The thing is, Alice and I couldn't find out anything about cheese and bights. We're going to ask Tommy Tucker for help tomorrow. Ugh. What if he teases us?"

Twinkles twitched his nose and looked at her with his beady black eyes. "He won't laugh. I think this will make him feel important and needed. Besides, how could he possibly resist one of your dad's **TOP SECRET SUPER DUPER CHALLENGES**?"

Twinkles had a good point. She and Alice always looked forward to these challenges. It was a bummer when Dad was at sea for long periods, but these challenges kept her so busy that the time seemed to fly by.

Twinkles scurried along her leg and startled her. "Um, did you forget about that snack you were going to get me?"

Abbey chuckled and headed to the kitchen to get some alfalfa sprouts from the fridge – Twinkles' favourite. While she was there, she had an idea. Why hadn't she thought of it before?

She raced upstairs to her mom's office, taking the stairs two at a time.

"Mom! Mom! I need a favour!" she yelled as she burst into the room.

"Whoa, slow down, honey. What's the favour?"

Taking one big breath, Abbey said "I was wondering if I could use your laptop to look up the two last words for the challenge. That would save me from asking Tommy Tucker for help tomorrow."

Her mother pointed to the empty desk beside her. "Sorry, Abbey, but my computer got a virus and I took it to the shop to be fixed. I won't have it back for a couple of days."

Bad luck again!

"Oh, okay," she said as she headed back down to her room slowly. She dreaded talking to Tommy Tucker tomorrow.

CHAPTER
9

TRICKY HELP

ABBEY DIDN'T SAY ANYTHING TO TOMMY Tucker on the bus. She was too nervous. She waited until they were in the school yard, when she and Alice could talk to him together. Abbey's mother had called this 'swallowing your pride', but Abbey thought it felt more like she had swallowed an elephant that was now doing sommersaults in her stomach. Ugh.

Alice spoke first. "Um, hi Tommy. We were wondering, I mean, maybe if you wanted to, you might be able to help us with something?" Alice sounded as nervous as Abbey felt.

To their surprise, Tommy didn't laugh at them or ignore them.

"What do you need *my* help for?" Tommy replied.

"Well, yesterday you said you were a knot expert. Is that actually true?" Abbey challenged.

Tommy nodded without saying a word.

Abbey gulped and continued, "You see, we have a secret challenge that involves knots, and we're kind of stuck. We thought you might be able to help us."

Abbey crossed her fingers behind her back, wishing for good luck. Tommy answered after a few moments.

"What do I get out of it?"

The girls glanced at each other before Alice said, "How about a share of the treasure?"

"Treasure? Now why didn't you say so! I'm in." Tommy said with delight.

After swearing Tommy Tucker to secrecy, Abbey and Alice told him all about the **TOP**

SECRET SUPER DUPER CHALLENGE, and what they had done so far. At the end of the tale, Tommy smiled. A big smile. A gigantic smile. A *friendly* smile.

"Do you have the smallest rope with you?" Tommy asked.

Abbey pulled it from her cargo pants that she was wearing again today. She planned on wearing them until they cracked this case.

Tommy took the rope and folded it in half.

"There you go. That's a bight."

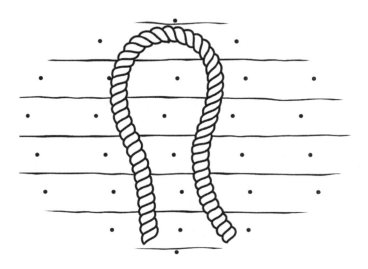

The girls stared at him as if he had just said that he had seen a unicorn.

"Funny joke, Tommy," said Alice, "now get serious."

"I *am* serious. The rounded part here is called the bight. My Dad and I spend a lot of time on our sailboat, so like I said, I know a thing or two about knots."

"But that's way too simple. It's not even a knot! My Dad wouldn't give us something so easy," Abbey protested.

Shrugging, Tommy said, "You can believe me or not, but it's still true. Check with your mom, and you'll see."

At that, Tommy turned and walked away, leaving the girls on their own for the rest of the day.

Abbey didn't really believe Tommy. How cruel he was to try to trick them like this. She imagined stuffing cotton balls up his nose. That made her feel better.

When she got home, Abbey took the folded rope to her mother.

"Is this a bight, Mom?" she asked in doubt.

"It sure is! Good job, that's two clues completed."

Abbey's good luck was back. But she knew she had to apologize to Tommy Tucker. Ugh.

CHAPTER 10

THE YELLOW BRICK ROAD

IT WAS DAY 3 OF THE **TOP SECRET SUPER DUPER CHALLENGE**. The girls felt confident. They only had one clue left to solve and it was only Wednesday. There was loads of time before Abbey's dad returned from sea on Friday.

They were going to apologize to Tommy this morning and get his help with the third clue. What could go wrong?

That's when disaster struck. Abbey's luck disappeared. Tommy wasn't at school that morning. He wasn't there at lunch, or in the afternoon either.

"What are we going to do?" Alice asked Abbey as the final bell rang.

"Let's not worry, I'm sure he'll be back tomorrow. He probably had a dentist appointment or something today. It will be fine. We still have two days."

The girls felt like they had wasted a precious day, but they were sure tomorrow would be better. Sort of sure. Okay, not really sure. Not at all.

The next day, things got worse. Mrs. Picard informed the class that Tommy had the *chickenpox* and wouldn't be back to school for a week. The girls groaned when they heard the news.

"A week? We can't wait that long!" Abbey exclaimed out loud. Everyone turned to look at her. She went red.

Mrs. Picard smiled and said, "Well, Abbey, if you're so concerned about Tommy, maybe the class should make him a get well card. I'll drop it off to him after school."

Abbey nodded. That gave Alice and idea.

She whispered to Abbey, "Psst. What if we put an extra note into Tommy's card to ask him to help us with the third clue?"

Together, they came up with a message that didn't give away the **TOP SECRET SUPER DUPER CHALLENGE**:

> Tommy,
> Sorry you're sick. Still need your help with the cheese.
> Call us, PLEASE!
> A+A   (728) 416-3324

After supper, the phone rang at Abbey's house. It was Tommy!

"Hello, Tommy?" Abbey answered nervously.

"Yeah, it's me."

Abbey wasn't sure how to begin. "How are you feeling? We missed you at school again today." At least that part was true, she thought.

"I'm pretty itchy actually. Being home in bed all day is boring. I never thought I'd miss school."

There was a long pause after Tommy stopped talking. Finally, Abbey asked, "I was wondering if you could help us with the *cheese* clue?" She held her breath, hoping Tommy would say yes.

"Oh, so *now* you believe me?" Tommy challenged.

Abbey felt bad. "Yeah, I'm really sorry about not believing you about the bight. You were right."

More silence.

Then, Tommy spoke up. "Think of the Yellow Brick Road. You know, from *The Wizard of Oz*?"

"I know the movie, but I don't get what that has to do with cheese or knots," Abbey admitted.

Tommy explained in more detail. "To cheese a rope, you hold the centre and twist the rest around and around in a tight spiral. At the end, it looks like a flat coil, just like the beginning of the Yellow Brick Road. Sailors use it to keep the lines looking nice and ordered."

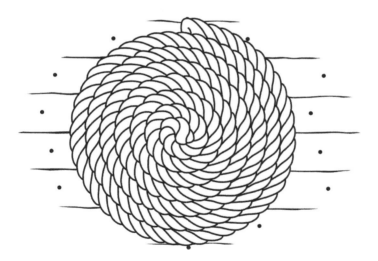

Abbey was impressed. "Thanks so much! I will give it a try. Alice will be so excited to know that we completed the third challenge. We owe you one Tommy!"

"You do remember that you promised to share the treasure, right?" Tommy asked with a cough.

"Of course! I'm going to ask Alice over tomorrow after school to show my mom the cheesed rope. If we're right, she'll give us the key to the box. I wish you could be here to open it with us."

"Maybe I can" Tommy said mysteriously as he told her about an idea he had.

CHAPTER 11

A FINAL SURPRISE

DAY 5. THE FINAL DAY. ABBEY HAD arranged for Alice to come over right after school to try cheesing the rope.

Mom was getting her laptop back from the shop, and she was certain that Skype with Tommy would work. Sometimes he had good ideas…for a boy.

When she and Alice got off the afternoon bus together, there was a surprise waiting for her.

"Dad!" Abbey yelled as she ran to him and wrapped her arms around him tightly. "I'm so happy you're home!"

On the walk to the house, Alice and Abbey told him about their adventure this week and about the plan for the final clue.

Dad smiled, "I can't wait."

At home, the girls went directly to Abbey's room to practice cheesing the rope before they showed anyone. Twinkles poked his head out of his tunnel and Abbey was pretty sure he winked at her.

It was finally time to take the rope to the living room, where Mom had set up a Skype call with Tommy on her computer. Tommy was smiling from ear to ear, even though he had red spots all over his face.

Abbey's parents were sitting on the couch.

"Okay, here's what we learned this week," Abbey began.

Before Abbey demonstrated, Alice added, "And we want to thank Tommy for helping us even when he was sick and when we didn't believe him!"

Tommy blushed on screen.

The girls first demonstrated a bight with the smallest rope. Following that, the medium-sized rope was tied into a perfect bowline first by Abbey and then by Alice. Finally, the girls got on their knees to cheese the longest rope.

Tommy interrupted once by saying "Just twist the centre a little tighter..." The girls smiled at him and did as he suggested. It looked perfect.

Once done, Abbey's parents applauded. Her father beamed. "I'm so proud of you all! You're ready to join the Navy," he joked.

"You've definitely earned this key." Abbey's mother added as she pulled a small, shiny key from her pocket.

The girls got the box, turned so that Tommy could see it on screen, and inserted the key. Abbey hoped that it wasn't cotton balls to shove up Tommy's nose.

"One, Two, Three!" Alice counted as Abbey turned the key with shaking hands.

Inside the box was a beautiful brass compass, showing the directions of North, South, East, and West in fancy letters. A small note was taped inside the lid:

Kathleen Thaler

For your next
Top Secret
Super Duper
Challenge

Dad smiled and said, "I guess you girls will have to get busy learning how to use a compass before I go to sea again. And that goes for you too, Tommy!"

Abbey and Alice happily agreed. It turns out that Tommy Tucker wasn't that bad after all, even if he was a boy…with chickenpox!

CPSIA information can be obtained
at www.ICGtesting.com
Printed in the USA
LVHW02s0408080318
569063LV00009B/34/P